Spider
waterSpout.
the rain
Spider out.
the Sun
all the rain.
Bitsy Spider
Spout again.

The Hugely-Wugely Spider

by **Ethan T. Berlin**

with illustrations by **Karl Newsom Edwards**

FARRAR STRAUS GIROUX/New York

The Itsy-Bitsy Spider
climbed up the waterspout.

And so did the Mitsy-Bitsy Spider.
And the Litsy-Plitsy Spider.
And the Witsy-Ditsy Spider.

Okay, basically all the spiders I know climbed up the waterspout. And they kind of implied that maybe I, the Hugely-Wugely Spider, was too big to climb up said waterspout. Whatever. I could climb up the waterspout if I wanted to! Which I don't!

Because who wants to climb up a waterspout that's filled with comfy webs, buckets of bugs, and piles of adorable leg warmers for all of my adorable legs?

Well . . . maybe I could try it.

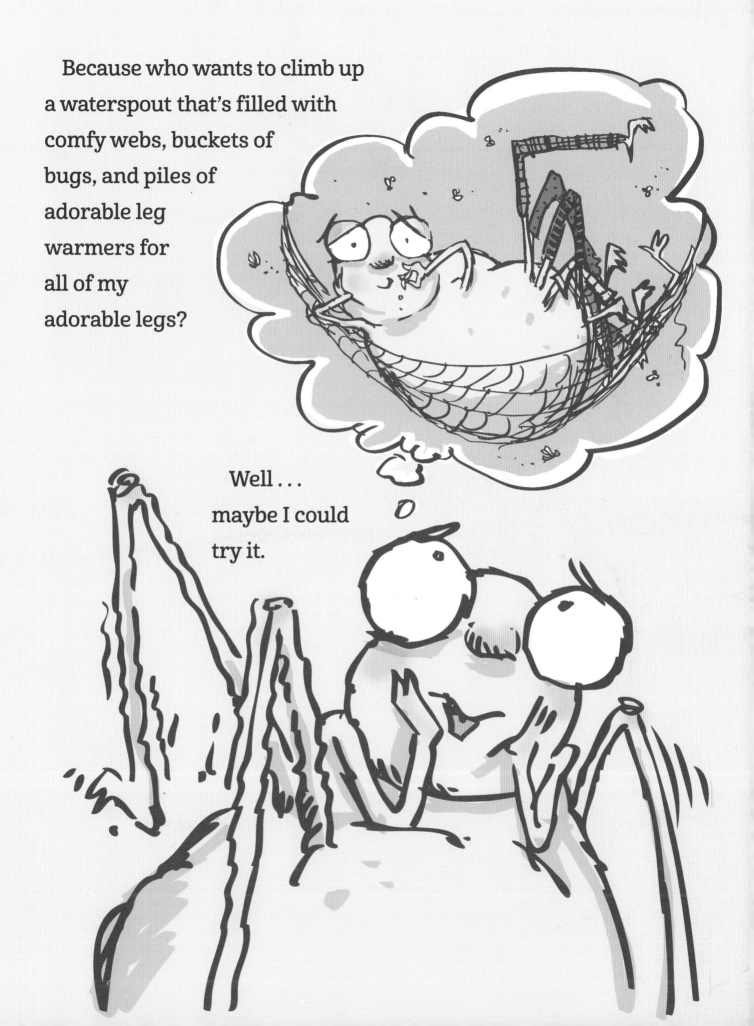

Hmm . . .

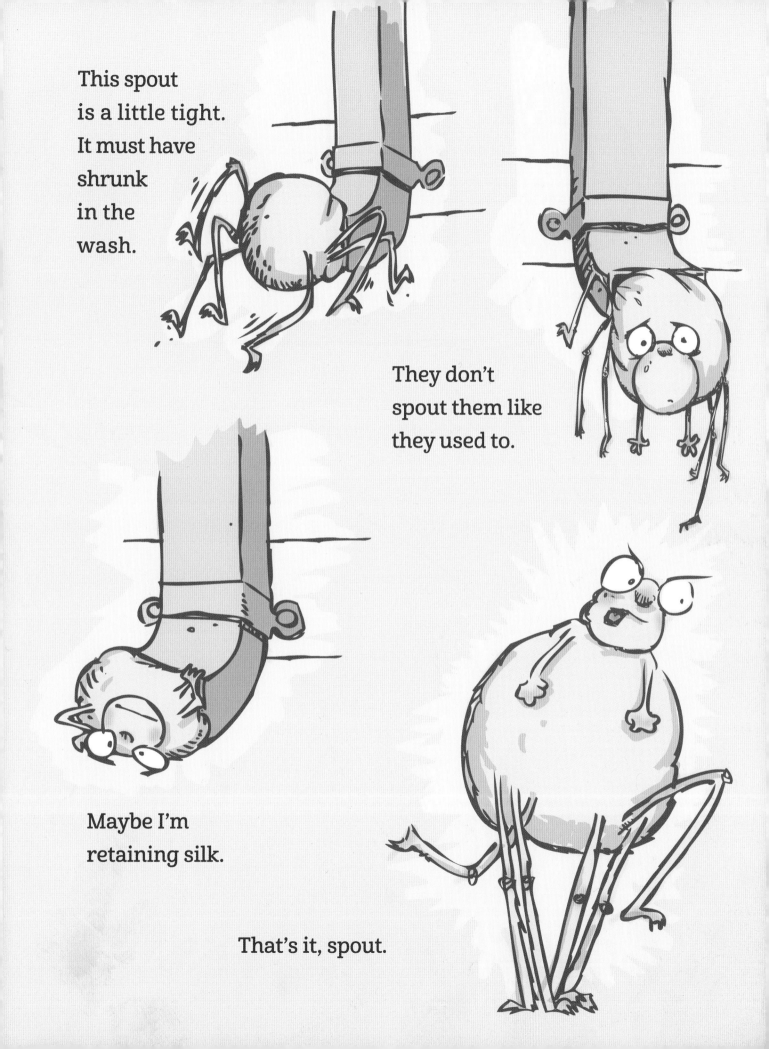

This spout is a little tight. It must have shrunk in the wash.

They don't spout them like they used to.

Maybe I'm retaining silk.

That's it, spout.

Okay, maybe I'm not a waterspout sort of spider. That's fine, they're kind of dangerous anyway because of all the . . .

Hey, guys,

weather's looking bad.
There's gonna be a lot more
water and a lot less spout!

Down comes the rain ...

AND WILL WASH
THE SPIDERS OUT!

Oh my gosh, look how slowly they run. They're so adorable. They're so itsy-bitsy. They're so . . .

IN TROUBLE!

Time to plug this spout!

Wow, lots of rain. And twigs. And acorns.

I did it!
I SAVED them!

Yay, out came the sun
and dried up
all the rain!

What?!

No! I dried up all the rain!
The sun didn't do anything.
It just stood there and got in
people's eyes!

It's true.

Really? You're just going to run away and not even thank me?! Do you know the personal sacrifices I made on your behalf? And the only thanks I get is . . .

. . . heaps and heaps of adorable leg warmers to keep all of my adorable legs perfectly warm!

And from that day on, the children
of the land sang a new song:

The Itsy-Bitsy Spider excluded the Hugely-Wugely Spider from the waterspout. And down came the rain, but the Hugely-Wugely Spider saved the day. Out came the sun and served no useful purpose. And the Itsy-Bitsy Spider realized he'd been bad at sharing spouts and gave the Hugely-Wugely Spider adorable leg accessories.

Okay, maybe nobody sings it but me.

For Kimmi, Ari, Milo, Mom, Dad,
Rebecca, Josh, and Gracie! —E.T.B.

To Joy and Anne: Together we made Hugely a hero!
—K.N.E.

Farrar Straus Giroux Books for Young Readers
An imprint of Macmillan Publishing Group, LLC
175 Fifth Avenue, New York, NY 10010

Text copyright © 2018 by Ethan T. Berlin
Illustrations copyright © 2018 by Karl Newsom Edwards
All rights reserved
Color separations by Embassy Graphics
Printed in China by Toppan Leefung Printing Ltd.,
Dongguan City, Guangdong Province
First edition, 2018
1 2 3 4 5 6 7 8 9 10
mackids.com

Library of Congress Cataloging-in-Publication Data

Names: Berlin, Ethan T., author | Edwards, Karl, illustrator.
Title: The hugely-wugely spider / Ethan T. Berlin ; illustrations
    by Karl Newsom Edwards.
Description: First edition. | New York : Farrar Straus Giroux,
    2018. | Summary: The hugely wugely spider tries to climb up
    the water spout like all the small spiders and, when he gets
    stuck, they help him out so when the rain comes, he tries to
    return the favor.
Identifiers: LCCN 2017042312 | ISBN 9780374306168 (hardcover)
Subjects: | CYAC: Spiders—Fiction. | Size—Fiction. | Rain and
    rainfall—Fiction. | Humorous stories.
Classification: LCC PZ7.1.B458 Hug 2018 | DDC [E]—dc23

LC record available at https://lccn.loc.gov/2017042312

Our books may be purchased in bulk for promotional, educational, or
business use. Please contact your local bookseller or the Macmillan Corporate
and Premium Sales Department at (800) 221-7945 ext. 5442 or by e-mail
at MacmillanSpecialMarkets@macmillan.com.

The Itsy-Bitsy
Hugely-Wugely Spider
And down came the
Wugely Spider saved
the Sun and Served
And the Itsy-Bitsy
been bad at Sharing S
Hugely-Wugely Spider